Why Was Daniel Scared?

Why Was Daniel Scared?

**by
Pauline Youd**

**illustrated by
Elaine Garvin**

Pauline
BOOKS & MEDIA

BOSTON

Library of Congress Cataloging–in–Publication Data

Youd, Pauline, 1932-
  Why was Daniel scared? / by Pauline Youd ; illustrated by Elaine Garvin.
    p.   cm.
  Summary: A simple retelling of the Old Testament story of Daniel in the lions' den, with an emphasis on the theme of trust in God.
  ISBN 0-8198-8282-8 (pbk.)
  1. Daniel (Biblical character)—Juvenile literature. [1. Daniel (Biblical character) 2. Bible stories—O.T.
I. Garvin, Elaine, ill. II. Title.
BS580.D2Y68   1996
224'.509505—dc20   96-22770
                                                                                                          CIP
                                                                                                           AC

Printed and published in the U.S.A. by Pauline Books & Media, 50 St. Paul's Avenue, Boston, MA 02130.

Pauline Books & Media is the publishing house of the Daughters of St. Paul, an international congregation of women religious serving the Church with the communications media.

1 2 3 4   99 98 97 96

Daniel lived in a town far from his home. The people who lived there didn't worship God. But Daniel loved God and prayed to him every day. He knew God was always with him even though his own family and friends could not be. Daniel knew God heard his prayers and would help him.

The king of the land where Daniel lived liked Daniel. Some of the king's officials noticed this. They grumbled, "The king likes Daniel better than he likes us." Others whispered, "Let's get Daniel in trouble."

The officials knew Daniel prayed to God, so they decided to trick the king into writing a law that made prayer to God a crime. The king signed the law, but Daniel still prayed to God.

The officials told on Daniel. They said he had to die because he disobeyed the new law. So the king had to put Daniel in the lions' den.

Was Daniel scared? The lions were big. They had strong jaws and sharp teeth. They were very hungry. Daniel looked like he would taste good.

What did Daniel do? He did what he always did when he was scared. He prayed and asked God to help him.

What did God do? He closed the lions' mouths so they couldn't hurt Daniel! (from Daniel 6).

In the story, Daniel loved God and prayed to him every day. That good habit helped Daniel later when he was in trouble.

Have you learned to pray? Remember, when you pray you are not just saying words. You are talking to God. God is always with you, so you can talk to him any time. God will always lead you in the right way. God hears you when you tell him you love him. God hears you when you tell him you're sorry. God helps you to be honest and brave when you're scared.

Pauline BOOKS & MEDIA

ALASKA
750 West 5th Ave., Anchorage, AK 99501   907-272-8183
CALIFORNIA
3908 Sepulveda Blvd., Culver City, CA 90230   310-397-8676
5945 Balboa Ave., San Diego, CA 92111   619-565-9181
46 Geary Street, San Francisco, CA 94108   415-781-5180
FLORIDA
145 S.W. 107th Ave., Miami, FL 33174   305-559-6715
HAWAII
1143 Bishop Street, Honolulu, HI 96813   808-521-2731
ILLINOIS
172 North Michigan Ave., Chicago, IL 60601   312-346-4228
LOUISIANA
4403 Veterans Memorial Blvd., Metairie, LA 70006   504-887-7631
MASSACHUSETTS
50 St. Paul's Ave., Jamaica Plain, Boston, MA 02130
 617-522-8911
Rte. 1, 885 Providence Hwy., Dedham, MA 02026   617-326-5385
MISSOURI
9804 Watson Rd., St. Louis, MO 63126   314-965-3512
NEW JERSEY
561 U.S. Route 1, Wick Plaza, Edison, NJ 08817   908-572-1200
NEW YORK
150 East 52nd Street, New York, NY 10022   212-754-1110
78 Fort Place, Staten Island, NY 10301   718-447-5071
OHIO
2105 Ontario Street (at Prospect Ave.), Cleveland, OH 44115
 610-621-9427
PENNSYLVANIA
Northeast Shopping Center, 9171-A Roosevelt Blvd.
Philadelphia, PA 19114; 215-676-9494
SOUTH CAROLINA
243 King Street, Charleston, SC 29401   803-577-0175
TENNESSEE
4811 Poplar Ave., Memphis, TN 38117   901-761-2987
TEXAS
114 Main Plaza, San Antonio, TX 78205   210-224-8101
VIRGINIA
1025 King Street, Alexandria, VA 22314   703-549-3806
CANADA
3022 Dufferin Street, Toronto, Ontario, Canada M6B 3T5
 416-781-9131